UNDER THE NORTH STAR

Also by Ted Hughes and Leonard Baskin

Cave Birds
Moon–Whales
Season Songs

UNDER THE NORTH STAR

TED HUGHES

DRAWINGS BY
LEONARD BASKIN

A STUDIO BOOK · THE VIKING PRESS · NEW YORK

First published in 1981 by The Viking Press (A Studio Book)
625 Madison Avenue, New York, N.Y. 10022

Published simultaneously in Canada by
Penguin Books Canada Limited

Library of Congress Cataloging in Publication Data
Hughes, Ted, 1930–
    Under the North Star.
    (A Studio book)
    1. Animals—Poetry.   I. Baskin, Leonard,
1922–   II. Title.
PR6058.U37U5   821'.914   80-17894
ISBN 0-670-73942-1

Printed in Japan by Dai Nippon Printing Company, Ltd., Tokyo
Set in Palatino

TH

To Lucretia

POEMS

AMULET

Inside the Wolf's fang, the mountain of heather.
Inside the mountain of heather, the Wolf's fur.
Inside the Wolf's fur, the ragged forest.
Inside the ragged forest, the Wolf's foot.
Inside the Wolf's foot, the stony horizon.
Inside the stony horizon, the Wolf's tongue.
Inside the Wolf's tongue, the Doe's tears.
Inside the Doe's tears, the frozen swamp.
Inside the frozen swamp, the Wolf's blood.
Inside the Wolf's blood, the snow wind.
Inside the snow wind, the Wolf's eye.
Inside the Wolf's eye, the North Star.
Inside the North Star, the Wolf's fang.

UNDER THE NORTH STAR

THE LOON

The Loon, the Loon
Hatched from the Moon

Writhes out of the lake
Like an airborne snake.

He swallows a trout
And then shakes out

A ghastly cry
As if the sky
Were trying to die.

THE WOLVERINE

The gleeful evil Wolverine
    Lopes along.
"O I am going to devour everybody and everything!"
    Is his song.

With gloating cackle the glutton gobbles
    The Eagle's brood.
Snaps the sleeping Snowy Owl's head off, chuckling
    "This is good!"

The trapped Wolf's pelt will not adorn
    The trapper's wall—
The Wolverine's swallowed it with a wild laugh
    Trap and all.

When he bobs up in the Northern Lights
    With more merry tales
The Bear feels the skull creak under his scalp
    And his smile fails.

The gleeful evil Wolverine
    Belly full of song
Sings: "I am coming to swallow you all, hiya!"
    Loping along.

THE SNOWY OWL

Yellow Eye O Yellow Eye
Yellow as the yellow Moon.

Out of the Black Hole of the North
The Ice Age is flying!

The Moon is flying low—
The Moon looms, hunting her Hare—

The Moon drops down, big with frost
And hungry as the end of the world.

The North Pole, rusty-throated,
Screeches, and the globe shudders—

The globe's eyes have squeezed shut with fear.
But the stars are shaking with joy.

And look!

The Hare has a dazzling monument!
A big-eyed blizzard standing

On feet of black iron!
Let us all rejoice in the Hare!

Snowy Owl O Snowy Owl
Staring the globe to stillness!

The Moon flies up.

A white mountain is flying.

The Hare has become an angel!

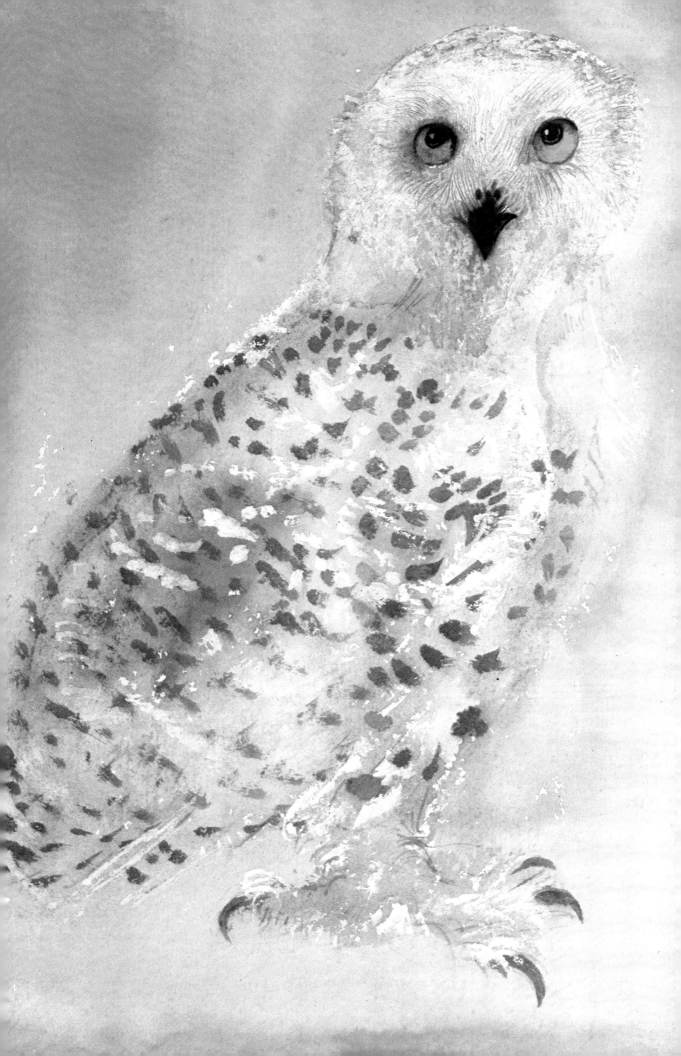

THE BLACK BEAR

The Bear's black bulk
Is solid sulk.

He mopes with his nose
Between his toes

Or rears with a roar
Like a crashed-back door
Shouting: "God swore

I'd be Adam—
And here I am

In Paradise!"
But then his eyes

Go pink with rage:
"But I am in a cage

Of rough black hair!
I have to wear

These dungfork hands!
And who understands

The words I shout
Through this fanged snout?

I am God's laugh!
I am God's clown!"

Then he glooms off
And lays him down

With a flea in his ear
To sleep till next year.

AN EVENING SEAL

Under fingers of blood
The islands dripped red
But the Clams in their bared bed
Gasped with blue cold.

And the Seal there, the Seal 0
She raised her oiled head.
My fingers had died.
But the Seal's wake sliced open

A serpent of crestings—
Unscrolling a long gash
In ocean's ripe flesh

As robed in her silks
She plunged with her razors

Under cold of such steel
I was frightened to feel.

THE MUSKELLUNGE

An interplanetary torpedo
Fell into the lake long ago
When worlds were being made.

Now he searches the abyss
With the hunger of a sun of ice.

Muskellunge hid his soul, where it's safe,
In the middle of the earth.
Then took a job with the lake
As jaws
For the hunger of sunk bedrock.

When the Heavens fell, this old witchdoctor
Rescued all the gods in one bag
And swallowed it. He has them safe in his belly.
Now he eats only for them.

There he lies
Wiser than Orion and older than the Great Bear

Waiting for the ages to pass.

A LYNX

The hushed limbs of forest,
Of clouds, of mountains, here
Take their hard-earned rest
Under the Lynx's ear.
In his sleep, they sleep—
As in a deep lake—deep.

Do not disturb this beast
Or clouds will open eyes,
Soundless the forest
Will fold away all its trees
And hazy the mountains
Fade among their stones.

THE SNOW-SHOE HARE

The Snow-Shoe Hare
Is his own sudden blizzard.

Or he comes, limping after the snowstorm,
A big, lost, left-behind snowflake
Crippled with bandages.

White, he is looking for a great whiteness
To hide in.
But the starry night is on his track—

His own dogged shadow
Panics him to right, and to left, and backwards,
    and forwards—
Till he skids skittering
Out over the blue ice, meeting the Moon.

He stretches, craning slender
Listening
For the Fox's icicles and the White Owl's slow cloud.

In his popping eyes
The whole crowded heaven struggles softly.

Glassy mountains, breathless, brittle forests
Are frosty aerials
Balanced in his ears.

And his nose bobs wilder
And his hot red heart thuds harder

Tethered so tightly
To his crouching shadow.

WOODPECKER

Woodpecker is rubber-necked
   But has a nose of steel.
He bangs his head against the wall
   And cannot even feel.

When Woodpecker's jack-hammer head
   Starts up its dreadful din
Knocking the dead bough double dead
   How do his eyes stay in?

Pity the poor dead oak that cries
   In terrors and in pains.
But pity more Woodpecker's eyes
   And bouncing rubber brains.

THE MUSK-OX

Express blizzards rumble, a horizontal snow-haulage,
Over the roof of the world.
The weathercock up there
Is the Musk-Ox, in his ankle-length hair.

Inside the skyslide steep continent of white darkness,
    under walloping wheels of wind,
He clings to his eyes—
A little castle with two windows
Like a fish on the bed of a flood river.

The stars are no company.
They huddle at the bottom of their aeons, only just
    existing,
Jostled by every gust,
Pinned precariously to their flutters of light,
Tense and weightless, ready to be snatched away into some
    other infinity.

And the broken tree-dwarves in their hollow, near him,
Have no energy for friendship, no words to spare,
Just hanging on, not daring to think of the sucking and
    bottomless emptiness of the blast
That grabs at their nape, and pounds their shoulders.

And the mountains stare towards them fadingly
Like solid-frozen mammoths staring at a Coca-Cola sign.
And the seas, heaping and freezing, neighbour him
    unknowingly
Like whales
Shouldering round a lost champagne cork.

He's happy.
Bowed beneath his snowed-under lean-to of horns,
Hunched over his nostrils, singing to himself,
Happy inside there, bent at his hearth-glow
Over the simple picture book
Of himself
As he was yesterday, as he will be tomorrow

While the Pole groans
And skies fall off the world's edge and the stars cling
    together.

THE HERON

The Sun's an iceberg
In the sky.
In solid freeze
The fishes lie.

Doomed is the Dab.
Death leans above—

But the Heron
Poised to stab
Has turned to iron
And cannot move.

THE GRIZZLY BEAR

I see a bear
Growing out of a bulb in wet soil licks its black tip
With a pink tongue its little eyes
Open and see a present an enormous bulging mystery
    package
Over which it walks sniffing at seams
Digging at the wrapping overjoyed holding the joy off
    sniffing and scratching
Teasing itself with scrapings and lickings and the thought
    of it
And little sips of the ecstasy of it

O bear do not open your package
Sit on your backside and sunburn your belly
It is all there it has actually arrived
No matter how long you dawdle it cannot get away
Shamble about lazily laze there in the admiration of it
With all the insects it's attracted all going crazy
And those others the squirrel with its pop-eyed amazement
The deer with its pop-eyed incredulity
The weasel pop-eyed with envy and trickery
All going mad for a share wave them off laze
Yawn and grin let your heart thump happily
Warm your shining cheek fur in the morning sun

You have got it everything for nothing

BROOKTROUT

The Brooktrout, superb as a matador,
Sways invisible there
In water empty as air.

The Brooktrout leaps, gorgeous as a jaguar,
But dropping back into swift glass
Resumes clear nothingness.

The numb-cold current's brain-wave is lightning—
No good shouting: "Look!"
It vanished as it struck.

You can catch Brooktrout, a goggling gewgaw—
But never the flash God made
Drawing the river's blade.

THE WENDIGO

The Wendigo's tread
Is a ghostly weight
On top of the head.

His footprints go deep
Through the nightmare drifts
Of the trapper's sleep

The Wendigo creaks
From trap to trap
And releasing the shrieks

The trapped corpse felt
He drinks up its soul
Leaving only the pelt

So the Wendigo swells
With a storm of souls
And their dying yells.

On a snow lake, soon,
The trapper shall stare
At the sudden Moon

And know his life's done
As the Wendigo sweeps
Through his skeleton

Like an owl of wind
With the blizzard wraiths
Of the creatures he skinned

Snatching his soul
To the shuddering lights
That fly with the Pole.

THE OSPREY

The fierce Osprey
Prays over the bay.

God hides below
In his shadow.

Let God reveal
His scaly, cold
And shining brow—

Osprey shall fold
His wings and bow
His head and kneel.

MOOSES

The goofy Moose, the walking house-frame,
Is lost
In the forest. He bumps, he blunders, he stands.

With massy bony thoughts sticking out near his ears—
Reaching out palm upwards, to catch whatever might be
    falling from heaven—
He tries to think,
Leaning their huge weight
On the lectern of his front legs.

He can't find the world!
Where did it go? What does a world look like?
The Moose
Crashes on, and crashes into a lake, and stares at the
    mountain, and cries
"Where do I belong? This is no place!"

He turns and drags half the lake out after him
And charges the cackling underbrush—

He meets another Moose.
He stares, he thinks "It's only a mirror!"

"Where is the world?" he groans, "O my lost world!
And why am I so ugly?
And why am I so far away from my feet?"

He weeps.
Hopeless drops drip from his droopy lips.

The other Moose just stands there doing the same.

Two dopes of the deep woods.

THE ARCTIC FOX

No feet. Snow.
Ear—a star-cut
Crystal of silence.
The world hangs watched.

Jaws flimsy as ice
Champ at the hoar-frost
Of something tasteless—
A snowflake of feathers.

The forest sighs.
A fur of breath
Empty as moonlight
Has a blue shadow.

A dream twitches
The sleeping face
Of the snow-lit land.

When day wakes
Sun will not find
What night hardly noticed.

PUMA

God put the Cougar on the Mountain
To be the organist
Of the cathedral-shaped echoes.

Her screams play the hollow cliffs, the brinks
And the abyss.
Her music amazes the acoustics.

She lifts the icy shivering summit
Of her screech
And climbs it, looking for her Maker.

A crazy-gaze priestess of caverns—
All night she tries to break into heaven
With a song like a missile, while the Moon frosts her face.

All day afterwards, worn out,
She sleeps in the sun.

Sometimes—half-melted
In the sheet-flame silence—
Opens one jewel.

SKUNK

Skunk's footfall plods padded
  But like the thunder-crash
He makes the night woods nervous
  And wears the lightning-flash—

From nose to tail a zigzag spark
  As warning to us all
That thunderbolts are very like
  The strokes he can let fall.

That cloudburst soak, that dazzling bang
  Of stink he can let drop
Over you like a cloak of tar
  Will bring you to a stop.

O Skunk! O King of Stinkards!
  Only the Moon knows
You are her prettiest, ugliest flower,
  Her blackest, whitest rose!

GOOSE

The White Bear, with smoking mouth, embraces
All the North.
The Wild Goose listens.

South, south—
                    the Goose stretches his neck
Over the glacier.

And high, high
Turns the globe in his hands.

Hunts with his pack from star to star.
Sees the sun far down behind the world.

Sinks through fingers of light, with apricot breast,
To startle sleeping farms, at apple dawn,
With iceberg breath.

Then to and fro all Christmas, evening and morning,
Urging his linked team,
Clears the fowler's gun and the surf angler.

Homesick
Smells the first flower of the Northern Lights—

Clears the Lamb's cry, wrestles heaven,
Sets the globe turning.

Clears the dawns—a compass tolling
North, north.
                    North, north.

Wingbeat wading the flame of evening.

Till he dips his eyes
In the whale's music

Among the boom
Of calving glaciers

And wooing of wolves
And rumpus of walrus.

41

WOLF

The Iron Wolf, the Iron Wolf

Stands on the world with jagged fur.
The rusty Moon rolls through the sky.
The iron river cannot stir.
The iron wind leaks out a cry

Caught in the barbed and iron wood.
The Iron Wolf runs over the snow
Looking for a speck of blood.
Only the Iron Wolf shall know

The iron of his fate.
He lifts his nose and moans,
Licks the world clean as a plate
And leaves his own bones.

THE MOSQUITO

To get into life
Mosquito died many deaths.

The slow millstone of Polar ice, turned by the Galaxy,
Only polished his egg.

Subzero, bulging all its mountain-power,
Failed to fracture his bubble.

The lake that held him swelled black,
Tightened to granite, with splintering teeth,
But only sharpened his needle.

Till the strain was too much, even for Earth.
Winter sank to her knees.

The stars drew off, trembling.
The mountains sat back, sweating.

The lake burst.

Mosquito

Flew up singing, over the broken waters—

A little haze of wings, a midget sun.

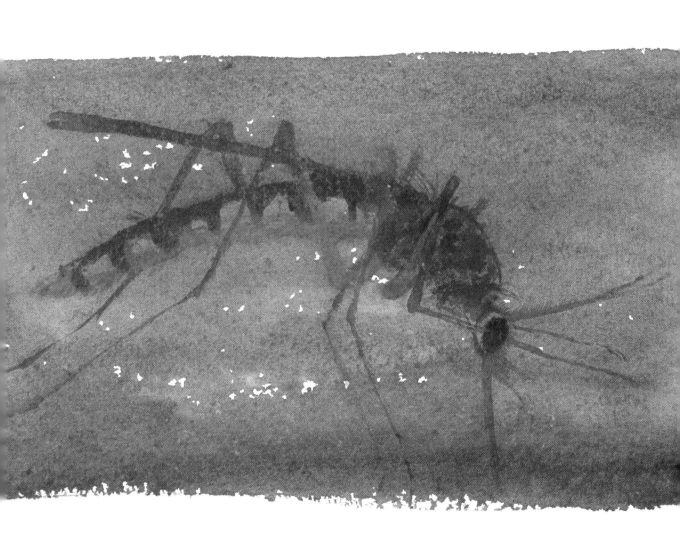

E AGLE

Big wings dawns dark.
The Sun is hunting.
Thunder collects, under granite eyebrows.

The horizons are ravenous.
The dark mountain has an electric eye.
The sun lowers its meat-hook.

His spread fingers measure a heaven, then a heaven.
His ancestors worship only him,
And his children's children cry to him alone.

His trapeze is a continent.
The Sun is looking for fuel
With the gaze of a guillotine.

And already the White Hare crouches at the sacrifice,
Already the Fawn stumbles to offer itself up
And the Wolf-Cub weeps to be chosen.

The huddle-shawled lightning-faced warrior
Stamps his shaggy-trousered dance
On an altar of blood.